# EYES SHUT

# EYES SHUT

## AND OTHER STORIES

### DANIELLE EPTING

*atmosphere press*

# Contents

# Author's Note

The following stories have been written over the past several years, the most recent as little as a year ago. Each is a work of fiction, although all fiction begins somewhere, usually embedded in the truth. As we know, the truth holds many different meanings for people and over time often becomes tangled in our own memories. Things become harder to remember, and it becomes more difficult to clearly decipher what happened.

I have used many of my own emotions to inspire the character's emotions in this collection. I also have drawn on traits of people I have met to give life to the characters; however, all events in the stories are fictional.

I feel my experiences have granted me the ability to write this collection and for that I am grateful. I find that I often enjoy reading story collections more than novels, only because there feels like several new beginnings within one book. Each story wraps up in its own way then the reader gets to move on to the next. I believe collections of stories are important reminders that there always is and always will be a next thing in our lives, regardless of how the previous ended.

The title, *Eyes Shut*, holds the same name as the final story. Many of the characters in this collection are blind to both the good and bad that they encounter as I feel many of us are, myself included. We are often unable to see what is right in front of us until it is either gone or too late to change.

All the stories in this collection are written for the person whom I've been writing much of my work about since I started, perhaps in the selfish hope that one day, they may open their eyes too.

## Where You Will Find It

He bought her a dog. It was one of those small, wiry ones that never stops shaking. It was an ugly dog, and it often woke her up at two in the morning only to go outside and howl. And every time she heard the howling, she would run outside to figure out what all the fuss was about, and that dog would just be standing in the middle of the yard, barking at nothing at all.

It was an apology dog. It was an "I'm sorry for leaving you" dog. And she did not want a dog.

She named it Whitney Houston. Because to her, the howling sounded like the "You-oo-ooo" in the real Whitney Houston's song, "I Will Always Love You."

"Couldn't you have named it something else like Toto? It looks a bit like Toto from *The Wizard of Oz*," he said.

"I should have named it Shaky," she said.

She had often thought that she loved him. In the cold early hours of his bedroom while she lay awake listening to the sound of his snoring like a spoon caught in the garbage disposal, she thought to herself, *Yes, this is it. This is love. I will sit here listening to his sound and that will be enough.*

And even when he left her, returning to his wife and two daughters, she had still thought that she loved him. He told her, "I need to finish this relationship before beginning another."

*Relationship.* She said the word over and over to herself. It echoed in her mind like a prayer. She said it quietly in indistinct places. She yelled it out her car window on the morning commute to work. She said it slowly, enunciating it precisely. Re-la-tion-ship. She swirled the word around in her mouth, tasting each syllable with her tongue. came back to her only days later, clutching Whitney Houston under his right arm, to tell her he was definitely ready for a relationship with her and her only, and the word rang in her ears like the sole answer to her prayers.

She had often thought that he loved her too. She felt it when he left for work early in the morning and kissed her cheek softly, always twice, and then made his way to teach English at the school in town. When he left, she felt nothing but the silence in his apartment melding with the silence inside of her, closing in on her like an early grave.

There was a hamster named Arnold in his apartment. It was his youngest daughter's. His wife didn't allow pets in the house, so when he moved out he permitted his daughter to have one.

Arnold squeaked throughout the night, creating soft melodies with his snoring. But in the morning, while she lay in bed listening to the echoes of her own loneliness, even Arnold entered into a respectful silence.

In bed, they talked about things like love and divorce. *Does he miss his wife? His children? Will their separation be final? How does someone erase the memories, the years, the time spent together?* He spoke little, listening to her questions and becoming quiet when they spoke of these subjects. Occasionally, he would speak like a prophet, with a newfound hope for love and his own life.

Their relationship held a sort of lacking quality to it. It was one of the most cherished qualities of their relationship to her. She searched for the lack. Was there anything to do about it? Where could it be hiding? Certainly not in a dog.

She had once asked him if he loved her. It was something she immediately regretted. He was very still for a moment and then began to give her the definition of the word love. She stared at him while he defined the word in every possible way. Often when she would stare at him, she would find that he in turn was staring at nothing at all, maybe the bookcase, or the bed, or out the window. In fact, he had a hard time meeting her gaze, but still her eyes clung to him. She felt that she stuck to him. Their relationship had a sticky consistency; she clung to him so as not to consider anything else.

He told her the origin of the word love: Old English *lufu,* of Germanic origin, or from the Latin words *lubere* or *libere,* meaning "to please." He said it slowly, enunciating it precisely. Love. He swirled the word around in his mouth, tasting it with his tongue. "L-o-v-e," he said. "What is it good for?"

Over coffee and blueberry muffins, while the heavy snow barreled down outside, her friend Lisa told her she was behaving as if she were a "naive woman." Lisa removed only the top off her blueberry muffin and ate it in small pieces like a bird picking at seeds on the ground. "Surely you must see it," Lisa said.

She felt like she was wasting. Wasting time, wasting away, wasting her good skin and boobs. God! Those boobs! They would never again stand so as they did right now and she was wasting them on him. He would lay face down on top of her, his head nestled between her boobs, and she would think, *Is this what they have gone to use for?* She scratched the back of his head like a dog, the way she scratched behind Whitney's ears, counting his gray hairs like lost moments of her life.

Sometimes they met at restaurants. She ordered and ate small, simple salads of spinach, cucumbers, craisins. He ordered large meals: ribs with fries or steak with vegetables and potatoes. He was hungry all the time, eating meals no matter the hour of the day as if he could not get enough. He would joke at her plate of "leaves," he called them, though she rarely felt hungry when she was with him. They could spend hours, days together and she felt she did not need to eat. The thought of eating a tenderloin or a chicken breast was unimaginable.

He had been in an excruciatingly good mood lately and it made her nervous. He had a normal, miserable air about him that seemed to be gone, and she was struck with a sudden fear that he would leave her.

At the end of their time together, he always said, "It was good seeing you," as if it would be the last time, which she often thought it was. She would prepare herself for his leaving, for the loneliness, perhaps for another dog. She examined everything: his words, the quick, short movements of his body, her spinach.

And when she didn't hear from him for some time, she would begin to burrow deep down into herself like a sand crab, devoting her life to nothing but the flow of the tide in order to remain shallowly buried in the wash of the waves. But when he called once again, she seemed to dig herself out of the deceiving refuge of the sand and float away with him.

She had met his youngest daughter once. His daughter had his eyes and hair. It was startling to see another version of him. His daughter ate chicken tenders and threw her fries across the table at her father. He grew angry. When he was angry, his right eyebrow scrunched up, giving him a quizzical look as if he could not believe what was happening.

*Was this love?* To examine someone so, to spend so much time on one look, one expression. She stared back at his quizzical look, back at that eyebrow. He was never-changing. And maybe this is what led to her loneliness, her inability to reach him, to find what it was that grounded him to his world when for her, it had always been him.

The last time he kissed her cheek twice in the morning, she imagined he told her that he loved her. She pretended he said this with a tone of undeniable truth and she smiled violently. He whispered to her that he would not be able to see her for some time, that he would be very busy with work and his children. She nodded, eyes still closed, basking in the words he never said.

Weeks passed and she did not see or hear from him. She drank coffee and ate muffins with Lisa to discuss his disappearance nearly every day. "What if something happened to him?" she asked. "There is no way for me to know." Lisa shook her head and finished the top of her muffin.

She was out walking Whitney in town when she saw him crossing the street with his wife and daughters. He looked at her indistinctly for only a moment as if she were someone he faintly recognized from his past but could no longer place. His youngest daughter was crying and holding his wife's hand. She thought of calling out to him, screaming like a madwoman would. She imagined the expression on his wife's face, the recognition of another lover, someone else in her husband's life. She watched as he crossed the street to his car. She stood outside the CVS, clutching Whitney's leash and poop bag. He buckled his children into the backseat and drove away from her.

Two months passed. He wasn't answering his phone and she wasn't getting her period. Lisa told her she should schedule an appointment. In the doctor's office, Lisa held her hand while the doctor told her she was pregnant. Lisa cried. The ultrasound was nothing more than a tiny shadow and it reminded her of Arnold, all balled up and calm in the early hours of the morning. "You don't have to make a decision right away," said the doctor.

More weeks passed. Too many weeks passed. The decision was made for her. He still wasn't answering his phone. The thought of leaving the news on his voicemail made her entire body ache. She did not tell him. She went back to the doctor. The ultrasound no longer looked like a hamster now but like something else entirely. *Could this be it?* she wondered. Lisa was holding her hand. The doctor told her she was having a girl. She thought of him then for only a moment and of the loneliness inside her that she now struggled to find. She thought of the uncertainty that had once made her feel most alive and how she had come to hate it. She felt something else now within her. A new source of strength, rising from inside, bursting through her skin like a hopeful energy. *Now this*, she thought, *this is something I can love.*

# Extraction

The only girl I had ever loved and been with began cheating on me after three years together, and I kept the knowledge of her affair to myself for months. I knew it was the sort of thing that you can't come back from, not really anyway.

At the time, I was a writer for an emerging online magazine about "life experiences"; sexual experiences to be more specific. I had been something of a slut before meeting Jacqueline. I mostly dated boys, a few girls, but I was never with them. That is, I never actually had sex with a woman until Jacqueline. It completely changed everything for me. I had never thought of myself as gay. I knew I liked women, something about their smell and the way their lips would spread across their teeth when they smiled, but gay was something different.

Jacqueline had long, curly black hair. It matched her every movement, sometimes a step ahead of her body. I always thought she must really trust her hair. Hair like that takes work, but she looked flawless.

The first time I met Jacqueline was at my friend's housewarming party. My friend Grace and her partner had just moved in together. There were lots of lesbians. And cats. So many lesbians and cats in one place. It's difficult to be gay and allergic to cats. I am very allergic to cats. I took possibly too much allergy medication before going to the party and still I couldn't stop sneezing. I always thought one cat per lesbian couple was plenty. But Grace always took things to her own level. They had six cats, and they would roam the house freely, greeting people and mingling as if they were the real hosts of the party.

Grace owned an art gallery in downtown Hudson. She had always said since we were kids that she wanted to leave New York, but in the end, she stayed. At the party she seemed so settled into her life, content with all her cats and her partner. She acted as if she never used to think that way at all.

Jacqueline knew Grace from college. Apparently, they had been in a history course together, forced to present a PowerPoint on the "Role of the Victorian Woman." They laughed wildly recalling the whole thing.

"Remember you wore that bright yellow poofy dress with the five-inch heels for the presentation?" Jacqueline asked.

"Yes! And the professor told me I was a disgrace to the Victorian Woman!" said Grace.

Grace was definitely not one to wear dresses. I actually could not recall a time I had ever seen her in anything besides pants or shorts. She liked to be comfortable, she said, and what the Victorian women wore was definitely not that.

Jacqueline had been late to the party, and I soon found out she was late to most things. She came flying in, those long black curls bouncing around, with a wide smile and bag of leftovers from a restaurant in hand.

"What the hell is that?" Grace asked.

"I brought you some leftover steak!"

"Get that away from me. What is wrong with you?"

I found Jacqueline strange and spontaneous. I was drawn to her. When she noticed me standing there, she said, "Want some steak?"

That night we talked until it seemed everyone else had left, Grace's cats still circling us. She asked if I wanted to go out to dinner sometime.

"Maybe have a fresh steak?" she said. "If you're into that sort of thing."

I had known from the moment I met her that I was definitely into that sort of thing.

Meeting Jacqueline was the beginning of an end for me. The end of my life searching for meaning in dicks and hairy men and the beginning of an even bigger heartbreak.

In the beginning, being with Jacqueline felt like a fresh opportunity for me, especially after moving back upstate and out of the city away from my boyfriend who said I would be perfect if I were just a little quieter, and who lied to me about having a family in Brooklyn with two kids, and who gave me Chlamydia, blah blah blah. In the end, I knew exactly why I moved back upstate.

For my job, I wrote blog articles about my "adventures" as if they were currently happening, and sometimes they were. Jacqueline knew this of course, and she knew I wasn't actually doing anything with anyone else. Any of the real sexual adventures I wrote about happened long before her. But for my job, I would download dating apps, swipe, go on a date, and just be there for the experience. I met some interesting people and they only added a little extra flair to my blogs. I wrote all sorts of things. Some of my most-read articles included, "The Insecure Hottie with the Micro Penis," "The Date with the Botanist Who Also Had Agoraphobia," and "The Sexy Barista with the Widow's Peak I Almost Married." The list goes on.

So when I discovered Jacqueline had been sleeping with someone else, I started stealing her Zoloft. She had a prescription that she renewed monthly, and she would never remember to take them every day so there was always some left. Her doctor kept telling her that she had to be consistent, she had to take them every day so the medicine could build up in her system.

It made sense why Jacqueline first started taking the Zoloft. She had a difficult job that she loved. She was a second-grade teacher for kids with disabilities and boy did she care about them. The kids and parents loved her so much. For holidays they would give her gifts and cards showing their appreciation for all she did. They knew her favorite chocolates, flowers, and they made sure she felt like she mattered. Jacqueline was a good person. I knew this. I kept telling myself this.

Well, the Zoloft wasn't building up in her system, but it sure was building up in mine. I was definitely taking it every day, almost at the same time actually. Every night after she would finish using the bathroom and brushing her teeth, I would take my turn. The first thing I did in that bathroom was pop a Zoloft. It was a sort of revenge, a passive kind of revolt.

I felt like I was stuck. I didn't want to make any sudden movements. The wrong move, the wrong word, anything felt like it could topple us. Our relationship was a house of cards and she didn't even know it. I wasn't ready for it all to fall yet. A decision had to be made but what if I didn't want to make that decision? *Who would move out?* I had nowhere to go. *Would she move in with her?* No. I definitely didn't want that either.

Instead, I let the Zoloft build up. I filtered my words after she came home from work so that I didn't reveal I knew she was with Lisa during her lunch break.

I was in the car with Jacqueline, driving to see my family on Christmas day when I bit into a chocolate chip granola bar, and I felt half of my molar remove itself, gently, from the rest of my tooth. I paused, with the chewed pieces of granola and half my molar on my tongue, not wanting to deal with it. I thought maybe if I sat still enough it would reattach itself. I know now that this was the true beginning of the Big Blowup.

I must have sat in silence for more than five minutes. I could feel Jacqueline sneaking glances at me from the driver's seat, wondering why I stopped eating. For the first time, I felt the Zoloft doing its thing. If I had not been on it, I am certain I would have screamed, cried, lost my mind. But I didn't. I just sat there knowing there was nothing I could have done to prevent it.

"Everything okay?" she asked. I nodded.

We came to a red light. She craned her neck to look at me directly. Her eyes were searching mine and I felt like a cornered animal.

"What's going on?" she asked.

Finally, I opened my mouth and fished out the piece of tooth. I held it up like a trophy, smiling.

"Ew!" she squealed.

Later, my dentist would tell me that tooth was always dying. It was rotting inside at its core, and I asked how they could have missed it.

"We just can't see everything on the x-rays," he explained. My dentist was an older man, mid-seventies, with a long, gray beard who probably should have retired years ago. Weeks later, he would be witness to the Big Blowup between me and Jacqueline.

*But how could this be*? I thought to myself. I had never noticed that tooth before. It never hurt at all, never gave me any real reason to acknowledge it. But the whole time it was rotten. I kept wondering how he missed it. *Isn't it his job?* I thought. *And isn't it my job*, I thought, *to know the person I'm sharing my life with?*

After the tooth fell out, there was just a jagged piece left behind in the back of my mouth. We still went to Christmas at my family's house and the tooth served as a talking point. My nieces and nephews loved Jacqueline just like the kids at her school did. She was kind and loving to them. She brought gifts and candy and told them how special they were.

I felt myself soften a bit for her, watching her help my three-year-old niece build up what seemed to be a hundred blocks and then knock them all down. Part of me wanted to run over and sit with them, put my arm around Jacqueline like I always would have, but what I really wanted to do was scream out, "Hey kids! Your Auntie

Jacky is actually a lying piece of shit!"

I had to wait several weeks until I could get the tooth out, and the jagged piece that was left behind would stick me in the gums every day. I complained about it, mostly just to Jacqueline. My dentist offered to smooth it down for me until the appointment when they would take the rest out, but I said no. I liked it. I wanted to feel the way it softly dug into my gum, sometimes making it bleed just enough that I could taste it.

I first knew something was wrong when I started with the sneezing. I was allergic to two things: pollen and cats. And it was winter.

Lisa had a cat. I was sure of it. *Where else would this cat fur be coming from?* I went mad. I checked the laundry. I scanned clothing for tiny hairs and found them. I picked them off of Jacqueline's work clothes, gym clothes, jeans, one by one, sneezing, coughing, sobbing, knowing something was happening.

Here's how I found out for certain: Jacqueline would no longer call me during her lunch break at work. This was strange to me. We were both busy people which I understood, but we had been calling each other at lunch for three years. There was an urgency to our relationship that was gone. The feeling of needing to speak to one another any chance we could no longer was there.

"We can just text during the day, and I'll see you at home after work," she had said. "We are both so busy."

I agreed.

Then one night while she was sleeping, I took her phone off the charger on her side of the bed. I used her limp, sleeping fingerprint to unlock the phone. I wasn't proud of it. I had never been that person in a relationship. But this felt different. *If I were to confront her, and she didn't deny it, what was I to say then?*

I opened her texts. Lisa was first in line, then my name. I clicked on my own name and read our last texts.

Jacqueline: *What's for din?*

Me: *The usual.*

We had veggie burgers with chips and salsa for dinner that night and I swear that I thought about not looking at her messages with Lisa, just locking the phone, plugging it back in, and going to bed. But I just stared at her name: Lisa. It didn't fit there. It was taking up space that did not belong to her.

I regretted it almost immediately. They had been texting all afternoon. At 4:45 p.m., fifteen minutes before Jacqueline came home, there was a photo. I opened it.

It was Lisa, standing in the middle of what I guessed was her living room, completely naked. She took the selfie from a high angle, holding the phone above her head. You could see her whole body, from her straight blonde hair, past her perky boobs and shaved vagina to her toes. I never shaved down there. Jacqueline had always said she liked it better that way.

Looking at the photo again, I saw something in the background. It was a brown and gray cat, perched on the sofa, looking just as startled by the photo as I was. I locked Jacqueline's phone and put it back on the charger.

Crawling into my side of the bed that night I felt like a stranger in my own home. I was a stranger to this life that she had without me. I didn't know the things she and Lisa shared with each other. *Did she share these same things with me still?* I felt so out of place, like there wasn't anywhere for me anymore. I don't think I slept one minute that night.

Life went on. I kept working and so did she, working right through lunch every day. I kept writing my stories and Jacqueline wrote her own with Lisa.

I wanted my blogs to be better, more interesting. If Jacqueline could live an exciting life, then so could I. So I put an ad out on craigslist that said "Female, white, mid-twenties, looking for an affair." I wasn't expecting the turnaround that it got. Over a hundred hits in a few hours. I decided on a man named Richard. We met for coffee and he told me he was a retired attorney who didn't believe in monogamy. He was much older than I imagined and said he was committed to only dating women below thirty.

He told me he liked the shape of my neck and asked if I would be interested in getting a real drink with him.

"Yes," I said.

"I knew you were one of them," he said, smiling.

I didn't know who "one of them" was and I still don't, but I left the coffee shop with him anyway and walked down the street to a bar. We had two martinis and he talked the entire time about the awful clients he had during his career and then told me he needed a cigarette. We stepped outside and he handed me one without asking if I smoked. He lit his first and then mine, then pushed me hard up against the brick wall of the bar. I gasped, dropping the lit cigarette before it even touched my lips. He wrapped his hand around my neck, and it felt too tight but also good, secure. I hadn't felt so secure in a long time.

"How long have you been with your husband?" he whispered into my ear. His hand was so tight around my neck I could barely reply.

Sensing this, he released his hand only slightly so I could get out the words.

"I have a partner," I said. "I've been with her for three years."

He released me immediately. He looked at me in disgust, spit, threw the rest of his cigarette at me, and walked away.

I once dated a man like Richard when I was living in the city. Our sex was amazing. He was tall and strong and intimidating to me in every way. We would fuck for hours, learn what made each other tick sexually, what drew us right to the edge before falling over. It was intimate in the shallowest of ways. He knew absolutely nothing about me. I wrote about him in my blogs for years. The kinky foreplay, almost angry desire for one another. But it was when the slapping and roughness in the bedroom turned into actual disdain that I knew it was time to go.

When Jacqueline and I first started dating, things were better with her. I found that being with her was easier, and not just because she was a woman, but because she was unapologetically herself. I just felt more like me, more comfortable. I used to obsess over everything before when dating: my clothes, hair, makeup. But our dates were different. We had unique dates: bird watching, the shooting range, running ten miles together.

Our relationship had always been active. Active mentally and physically, and that's how I knew it was really going south. We stopped all this. We stopped actively wanting to be around each other.

Jacqueline wasn't afraid of anything, and maybe this is why I was so afraid to confront her. She had a way of telling people what they didn't want to but needed to hear. Her sister had once gained weight after being let go from her job. I told her that she looked good, that she deserved to treat herself during a rough time. But Jacqueline told her she gained too much weight and needed to stop moping around.

"Life sucks sometimes," Jacqueline said. "It doesn't mean you give up and stop taking care of yourself."

Her sister was upset with her for a few weeks, but she did start running and discovered she loved it. She lost all the weight and more. Now, she runs in a race every other weekend and even ran her first marathon last month.

But I didn't want Jacqueline to be honest with me about something so hurtful that I already knew was true, even if I did need to hear her say it. I knew it was possible she would look at me and simply say: "Yes. I am sleeping with someone else. And she's better than you." I feared that she must desire something about Lisa over me, otherwise why would she do it?

In those last days before the Big Blowup, I started to wonder if she did love Lisa. She must have. She had to love her in some way, even love some part of her simply by being with her.

In the end, it really was the tooth that did us in. Jacqueline couldn't take it anymore. And honestly, I was being very dramatic about the whole thing. I continued to complain about it stabbing my gum, and I would only eat soft foods, terrified to lose the jagged piece.

"They are taking it out anyway!" Jacqueline said, during an argument over ordering Chinese food. I felt our usual order including crab rangoon and spring rolls would be too much for my tooth.

"So what?" I said. "I don't want another piece falling out."

"Oh my god. At least go have them smooth it out."

"It's not yours!" I yelled back, like a child.

When it was finally time to get the tooth out, Jacqueline took me to the appointment. I wanted to go alone, but she insisted. I made the appointment for the afternoon, and Jacqueline came straight from work still dressed in her work clothes.

They were going to give me "laughing gas." I would be awake during it, numb of course, but I would not really know what was going on. When she arrived, she hugged me, told me it would be over before I knew it.

I felt better with her there somehow, just knowing she was with me. She was smiling, holding my hand next to me in the chair. She knew how much I hated the dentist, how messed up my teeth were as a kid, and the horror stories I would tell her.

But then I started sneezing. I could smell the cat. That fucking cat. It was all over her. I could see the fur on her black trousers.

"Are you alright?" my dentist kept asking.

The dental hygienist was trying to get the mask on my face but I just kept sneezing. Even when they finally got the mask over my face, I was still sneezing. And laughing.

"Okay," said my dentist. "One last check, no other medications other than the allergy medication right?"

"Right," said Jacqueline.

"Nope!" I blurted out. Everyone turned to look at me. I was in hysterics. "I take Zoloft!"

I remember everyone looking a bit shocked, like they weren't sure whether or not to believe me.

"No she doesn't," said Jacqueline.

"Actually, I do!" I said, laughing. "I take *your* Zoloft!"

Jacqueline looked unsure. Even I felt nervous, sweating, but I still could not stop laughing.

"Have you been taking my Zoloft?" asked Jacqueline.

My dentist tried to intervene, his long beard looking extra bizarre to me, causing me to laugh harder. "Zoloft is okay for this minor procedure," he said. "The gas will be fine with that medication."

"Why would you do that?" asked Jacqueline, ignoring him entirely.

I was laughing so hard then that the dental hygienists had to hold me down. "Because you're fucking Lisa!"

Honestly, I don't remember much after that. Maybe they turned up the gas. Maybe they turned it down. But I remember Jacqueline leaving the room and the next thing I knew I was waking up and my tooth was gone for good.

I had never imagined a life with Jacqueline before, but after having her I couldn't imagine a life without her. She felt like a staple in my life, like one might have a staple in their diet. She was like the rice in my life. *Is it wrong to compare your partner to rice?* I am unsure. But she absorbed everything, made me feel whole, filled me completely. I didn't know how to be without her.

The rest of that day, I felt somehow better knowing that the secret was out. It was no longer stuck inside of me. Instead, I felt it poisoning the air, climbing the steps with Jacqueline as she brought me soup for dinner, seeping in and out the door as she came and went doing errands that night.

Maybe she will move out, or maybe I will. Maybe she will wake up one day soon, roll over and simply tell me she wants to be with Lisa. But she hasn't yet. Maybe I will wake up and scream, tell her to get out. But not yet.

That night, she plugged her phone into the charger and climbed into her side of the bed. She was playing music like she always did before we went to sleep, soft rock songs on shuffle that usually made me feel snuggly and safe but instead were making me feel nauseous.

"Turn that off please," I said.

"Okay." She rolled over and paused the music. "Better?"

"Yes." I heard nothing but the sound of my own breathing and Jacqueline's silence next to me. Then, a vibration from her phone on the nightstand, startling us both. I sat up in bed but couldn't see a thing. The room was dark. I could hear nothing except for the beating of my own heart; the hard, steady beating upon the sudden discovery of a stranger in my own home.

## The Cat

I met my wife at a funeral. She was wearing a bright red and white striped blouse with a brown skirt. She was standing behind everyone around the grave, shuffling the different prayer cards she got at the wake from the day before, collecting them like baseball cards.

I remember thinking she was tall, abnormally tall maybe. Once I moved through a few people to get a better look at her, I could clearly see her four-inch heels.

When we spoke for the first time, she told me she was there because the guy who "bit it" was her boss and the whole office had to go. I told her that the guy was my brother, and that he died from a brain aneurysm suddenly while at home eating dinner with his wife.

She snorted. "I'm so sorry," she said, while still laughing. Louise was that funny kind of smart. Confident, not afraid to say how she felt. She knew how to get to you, how to make you feel like you could say anything—even if you were at a funeral.

And then we fell in love.

Well, it didn't happen exactly like that, but that's not the story I want to tell anyway. After meeting my wife at my brother's funeral, we married and were together for thirty-seven years. She still wore those strange outfits with different pattern combinations, bright colors, really just anything that didn't match. She was beautiful, and I knew that since the moment I met her. I always wondered why she didn't dress more "normal" I guess I would call it, but that just wasn't her. She didn't need to. Beautiful wasn't something she did, it was just something she was.

But after a while, things started to turn. She stopped wearing her bright, eccentric outfits and she donated all her heels to the Salvation Army because she thought she was too old to wear them. We started to see more people we knew in the obituaries every day, and we were attending more funerals. But instead, we were attending them together.

I'm not sure exactly when it started, but it did. We weren't the same people we were when we first met. We used to do things together, now we did them alone. Louise used to love to run. We ran marathons together before the kids. Now, she never even took her running shoes out of the closet. But I still ran every morning. I couldn't imagine stopping.

Louise was rarely home, volunteering with the church, making herself busy. But I can't speak much for Louise, however, because I was never home either. With the both of us being retired, it seemed we were busier than ever.

But then there was the morning I came home from running and found the cat.

Our neighborhood then was relatively pet-free. A lot of older, grumpy neighbors surrounded us, and I didn't realize it at the time, but Louise and I were both almost seventy, and we were slowly becoming those old, grumpy neighbors ourselves.

I was out of breath, standing in the driveway of our home, panting like a dog when I looked up to our front steps to see a black cat with two different colored eyes perched at the bottom step.

"Louise!" I yelled into the house. "Louise!"

"What?" she asked, barreling outside in her robe.

I pointed to the cat two steps below her. The cat simply turned its head to look back at Louise as if she were interrupting something.

"Look at him!" she said. "So beautiful!" She reached out to pet him. He nudged his head into her hand, closing both his light brown and green eye.

It was a beautiful cat. I had never seen one like it before. I don't like cats, never have, but this one was different, and my wife fell in love with it immediately.

"Where did he come from?" she asked.

"He was there when I got back," I said.

Louise checked him for a collar to tell us where he came from, but there was nothing.

"Let's keep him," she suggested.

"Are you crazy? We have no idea where this thing has been."

"Thing?" she rolled her eyes and picked up the cat. "He is not just a thing!"

So we kept the cat. She took it to the vet to get its shots

and medicine. She bought it a collar, put our house phone number on it, and named it "Mir Mir" (short for Miracle, because she said he was her little miracle).

For a while, Mir Mir really was a miracle for Louise. She started bringing it everywhere, and it seemed ridiculous to her that I even dared to question keeping the cat.

There are a million different ways for a relationship to turn sour, but I never thought that a cat could be one of them. I watched my wife with this cat, treating it like it was sent to be with her and only her, and I couldn't help but wonder what she was thinking. It was like she had lost her sense. I couldn't even joke about the cat or say anything negative about it without her getting upset. I had once thought that my wife was both beautiful and smart. But you can't be both. At least not forever.

It was in the parking lot of the grocery store when the cat spoke to me for the first time. We were in the car waiting for my wife. She had run in quickly, to get one of those twirly string toys for the cat and said, "Watch him," and then locked us in the car together.

A woman with two young boys was walking out of the grocery store, pushing a cart full of bags. The older boy tripped the younger boy, and he fell on his face. The woman bent over to pick him up, and as she did I noticed the large size of her backside. It didn't match the rest of her body, and I couldn't help but stare as she grabbed the boy by his yellow puffy jacket and lifted him to his feet.

"Would you look at the rear end on her?" said the cat.

I jumped and spun around to see the cat sitting completely still in the backseat, blinking at me as if I had been the one who said it.

"What?" I asked the cat, expecting a response. But the cat said nothing.

"What!" I yelled. It was just sitting there, saying nothing. I jumped out of the car, made sure the cat was locked in, and waited for my wife to come back. The cat sat, looking at me through the window the whole time.

"What are you doing?" my wife asked when she came back.

"I just needed some air," I said. I waited until she got in the car first and handed the toy to the cat. He latched onto it and started playing with it. I got back in the passenger seat and carefully watched the cat in the rearview mirror playing with his new toy the whole ride home.

After we took the cat to the grocery store, it kept wanting to go outside, and I told my wife this would happen.

"If you take it out all the time, it will get used to it," I said.

It was strange, really. My wife started walking the cat like a dog. Every night after dinner she walked the cat. No leash, it just strode along next to her through the neighborhood. I thought the neighbors must think we had lost it.

After dinner one evening, my wife asked me to walk it. She said she wasn't feeling well, but that Mir Mir had to go outside, he really just has to every single day, and so I needed to take him.

"It's a cat," I said.

"Do it," she said. And that was it.

This was how many conversations with my wife went. Something always seemed to be missing as if we were speaking two similar, but distinct languages, and something kept getting lost in translation. Often times I wanted to say more, explain, scream out, do something. But it seemed no matter what I did, the reaction was always the same.

The cat stayed right next to me while we walked down the street. Its long claws were tip-tapping on the pavement. The sun was still out but starting to go down. This was my favorite time of the day when it was hard to tell whether it was the morning or the evening. My wife called it the "in-between" time when it could feel like anything might happen.

A couple was walking by us. The woman was staring at the cat.

"How cute," she said.

The man was overweight. His stomach hung over his belt buckle and he was sweating, trying to keep up with the woman. He also stared at the cat, then at me. I could tell he thought I was nuts. He did not mention how cute it was.

"Keep up!" she shouted at the man. She power-walked ahead, and he stumbled behind, sweating, and cursing under his breath.

"Isn't it funny," said the cat. "The fundamental basis of a relationship functions on the necessity of compromise, and yet it seems that no one is satisfied."

"What the hell did you just say?" I asked.

"I'm just saying," the cat continued, "you can be with a person all your life and watch the person you thought they were dissolve right before your eyes."

"That's it," I said. I picked up the cat and started to walk home.

"I really would prefer to walk," it said.

I put my hand over its mouth to shut him up, but it kept talking. I couldn't hear what he was saying, its words were muffled under my hand until it bit me.

"Ow!" I yelled and dropped it. My hand was bleeding; his teeth marks clear on my skin. The cat landed on his feet, said nothing more, and walked toward home.

The next morning, Louise woke me in a panic. She was leaning over me in bed, holding broken, rotted teeth in her hand.

"What is that?" I said.

"They are Mir Mir's teeth! I found them in the house."

Now I remember thinking this was strange. "That's not possible," I said. "He just bit me yesterday."

She scheduled an emergency appointment with the vet. She was afraid all his teeth might fall out if she didn't get him there right away.

The vet said there was some kind of infection in his gums. Something he had never seen before. He prescribed strong antibiotics and sent them back home.

Louise was a wreck over this cat, obsessing day and night.

I started running longer miles so I didn't have to think about or see that cat for a bit. But just like it did every morning, my run eventually ended and I found myself right back on the front steps where I first found the cat.

One morning, I came back and cooked up a good breakfast: bacon, pancakes, lots of syrup. Just how I liked it. I could just barely hear my wife stirring upstairs when

I heard the tip-tap of the cat's long claws on the kitchen floor. It sat right at the entrance to our kitchen, in between the doorway, looking at me as if waiting for me to do something.

I decided I would ignore it. I went through the morning paper, checked the obituaries like I always did and then looked at the horoscope. If I had anything lower than four stars I was not happy. I always took the horoscope seriously. The stars set my mood for the day.

I looked to Scorpio to see that I had a two-star day. I couldn't remember how long it had been since I'd had a two-star day, if ever.

"You're really gonna eat all that shit after a run?" said the cat.

I slammed the newspaper down on the table and stared at the cat. It was in the same place as before, blinking at me.

"I'll do whatever I want!" I screamed at the cat. The cat stared for a moment and then sprinted under the table. I felt his long claws scratch down the front of my leg.

"Ow!" I screamed out. I lifted the tablecloth to see the blood dripping down my leg into my sneaker.

My wife rushed through the door then, looking concerned.

"What's the matter?" she asked.

"That damn cat!" I said. "It scratched me!"

The cat came out from under the table and curled up on my wife's foot.

"I'm sure he didn't mean it," she said. "You're okay, right?"

After that, I knew for certain the cat had my wife. He had her on his side and there was nothing I could do about it. I cleaned up the scratch on my leg, had to bandage it really good. The cut was deep and it kept bleeding for hours.

But later that day, I found black claws laying around the house like a trail. They started in the kitchen and led out to the living room where the cat was sleeping on the bed Louise bought for him.

"What is going on with him?" Louise asked the vet again.

They did all sorts of tests, scans, bloodwork, but everything was coming back negative. The vet said he had no idea what was wrong with the cat, that this can often be the problem with taking in strays off the street. He thought it was some kind of infection, but he couldn't be sure.

But it was when he started throwing up blood that I told my wife we were getting rid of him.

"We can't leave him now," she cried. "We took him in to save him."

We argued for days over what to do with the cat. He continued on throwing up everywhere. Blood was staining our carpets, sofa, bedspread. The cat was rotting from the inside and there was no way for us to stop it.

Every night my wife would stay up with the cat, and I couldn't bear to see her do that to herself. It reminded me of when the kids were young, and one of them would have a nightmare, and she would stay awake all night rocking them back to sleep if she had to.

But this cat was killing her. We were both home way more than usual because we had to clean up after the cat, take care of it, feed it when it would eat anything.

One late night, after my wife had finally gone to sleep, I snuck my way downstairs. I crept slyly down our old, creaky flight of stairs, silently in the night.

The cat was in the living room, lying in its bed. I picked it up. The cat woke up right away and started twisting and screeching in my arms. I covered its face with my hand again and held down its legs. I carried it to the door.

It was erratic, squirming, and crying out. I felt a liquid in the hand covering its mouth and saw blood dripping onto my nightgown. I opened the front door and threw it out.

In the morning Louise searched everywhere for Mir Mir.

"Where could he have gone?" she said. She was running into each room of the house until she finally made her way to the back door to see that it was left open just a crack.

"We must have left the door open by accident," I said.

She insisted on looking for him. I drove us around the neighborhood a few times, but there was no cat to be found.

"He has a collar on," she said. "Someone will bring him back."

Days, then weeks went by and no one brought him back. Louise was sad for a while, too long, but after several weeks it seemed we both went back to our usual routines. We forgot about the cat and moved on. I felt good with what I had done. I felt that I had spared my wife some of the pain of seeing the cat die. I figured he just wandered off somewhere that night and died on his own.

Several weeks later, me and my wife went downtown for dinner together. We ate pasta and drank wine and I felt okay for a while. I had forgotten about the cat. We actually were going out for a nice dinner for the first time in a long time, happy just to be with one another.

But after a bit, I started to feel strange. I wasn't listening to my wife anymore. I was thinking about the cat. I reached for my wine glass and knocked it over. The red wine dripped down my hand onto my shirt sleeve.

"You can't get rid of me that easily," my wife said suddenly.

"What did you just say?" I asked her. She looked surprised, maybe scared, like she didn't recognize me in that moment.

"I said," she continued, "that you can get that out easily."

I drank a lot more wine that night and my wife had to drive us home. Usually, I sleep well when I'm drunk, but that night I couldn't even close my eyes.

It could have also been because I was hearing something outside our bedroom door. It was quiet, like a tapping. I ignored it for a while, trying to fall asleep. But the tip-tapping sounded like it was coming up the stairs. I got up out of bed and walked out of our room. I saw the cat standing at the top of our stairs, eyes glowing.

"Get out or I'll make you!" I yelled.

"Do it," he said.

The cat looked so sly, like he knew exactly what he was doing to me. I could see all his missing teeth, the blood dripping out of his mouth. His paws were missing claws, and the only ones left looked jagged and sharp.

"Get out!" I screamed and kicked the cat down the stairs.

The sound of the body tumbling down the stairs was too loud. There was a lot of banging and then a final thud as the body hit the last steps. I was breathing heavily. I had never felt so angry before.

I thought about when I first found the cat and how much my wife had loved it. I thought about how it had slowly destroyed us, and I thought about when I had first gotten out of bed to see what the noise was and how Louise wasn't in bed next to me.

I leaned over the top step. It was dark, and I was shaking. I could see a body at the bottom of the stairs. I flicked on the hallway light to illuminate the stairs. My wife's body was at the bottom, her head bleeding against the final stair, staining the carpet. The cat was gone, and the tapping noise stopped. Now only a silence filled the house, as if the cat had never been there at all.

# If One Afternoon Your Lover Says

It is three o'clock in the afternoon, and you are sitting on the couch reading *The Bell Jar* by Sylvia Plath. He tells you while wearing his old, orange t-shirt that says, "Life is Good." You stare at the wine stain on the couch from the night before and try to remember how many glasses you had. Two? Three? Did you spill the wine? You may feel sick after thinking of all the wine you did or did not spill.

Ask him how the stain got there, maybe he knows. He says that he does not know. He is rigid and serious and has been seeing someone else for how long? You decide it does not matter. Make him say the words. "I don't love you anymore," he says. Notice the wine stain is in the shape of a smiley face. You might not believe him at first. You feel as if the stain is mocking you. If you begin to feel angry at the stain, do not, under any circumstances, yell at the wine stain. Ask him if she is someone you know. He will say that she isn't.

Moving out will be easy. You never really liked this neighborhood anyway. You detest the loud music that always plays next door and the way the sun shines in at just the right angle, waking you up every morning. Collect everything you can. Do this in a dramatic manner, so he knows you are serious about leaving right this second. Think about taking your toothbrush with you. Instead, leave it in the aqua cup on the bathroom sink next to his. Later that night, you will regret not taking it.

In your new apartment, you will need help paying the rent. Put an ad on craigslist that says, "Wanted–roommate who will not be home often." Your new roommate decorates the apartment with lots of plants. Ask her what she likes about plants. She will say she doesn't really like them, but she likes the idea of them. They will die after a few weeks. You will be the one to throw all of them away.

Take up a hobby to fill your free time. Begin running around your new neighborhood. Walk most days, but try to run. Buy a pair of fancy running sneakers that you know will eventually live out their days in the back of your closet, alone and forgotten. When running around your neighborhood, begin to notice all the changes your neighbors are making to their houses. Notice who mows their lawn regularly and who doesn't. Feel as though you are acting a bit like a stalker. Remind yourself that good observation is a sign of a well-rounded individual.

Book a flight for your dream vacation because you have earned it. Spend two weeks in Hawaii swimming with dolphins, snorkeling for the first time, and hiking the Stairway to Heaven in Oahu. You may feel as though you've found yourself. Do not actually go on this vacation. Simply get a haircut instead. Dye it a fancy color and cut it short. Hate it. Vow never to do it again.

Register for a class in women and gender studies to better your understanding of the oppression of women in this patriarchal society. Your professor will wear strange outfits and talk about how many ex-husbands she has. She will ask questions like, "Why is it hard for women to recognize their own marginalization?" and "How do we begin to do something about it?" Drop the class.

On your way home after a long day browsing the organic food section in Walmart, you will see a stranger in the street and think it's your ex-lover. Duck behind the steering wheel of your car. Realize it's not him and feel ridiculous. You may even feel depressed.

Online, find a therapist whose specialty is "care of the soul and personal growth." At your first appointment, tell her you are going crazy. She will tell you that crazy people do not think they are crazy. She does, however, tell you that you are certainly neurotic.

Invite your mother over for dinner. Make her something to prove you are doing just fine, like eggplant parmesan or pecan-crusted chicken. She will ask how everything is, and you will say good. She compliments you on your cooking and asks for the recipe. You say you will send it to her. She wants to know if you will be keeping this haircut. She asks if she would be able to meet your roommate, but your roommate isn't home.

Your roommate continues to buy plants and hang them in your apartment. She wakes up every morning at six to do yoga and tells you it is time for you to get back out there.

She sets up a Tinder profile for you. In your bio, she writes, "looking for," then asks you what you are looking for. You will not know. She fills it in for you so that it will read, "looking for a good time." You swipe right on most of the profiles you look at. Or is it left?

Decide to go about this in a practical manner. Make it a project. You date men with the same names as the first ten presidents of the United States of America. This will not be difficult.

James Madison will be the first president you can find on Tinder. Arrive thirty minutes early to the restaurant. Five minutes before you are supposed to meet James, leave. There is a man outside the gas station next door smoking a cigarette. You have never smoked before. Ask if you can "bum a smoke." You will be unsure if you say it correctly. He will look you up and down before giving you a cigarette and ask you, "What do I get in return?" Decide to never smoke again.

Go back to the restaurant and apologize to your date for being late. He will assure you that it is no problem. He tells you that he is fluent in pig Latin and works as a professional juggler. You don't remember reading this about James Madison in your middle school history books.

Thomas Jefferson takes you to a fancy restaurant and orders your food for you. When the bill comes, he leaves an illegible signature. You can barely decipher his t's from his f's. You will be disgusted. How is he to declare the freedom of the thirteen colonies of America from Britain with handwriting such as that?

You go on the rest of your dates with the presidents, though you cannot find all of them. At your weekly appointment with your therapist, tell her you are getting back out there, but you will most definitely lose your mind if you cannot find your William Henry Harrison.

You leave your appointment and drive to all the places you used to go with your lover. Ex-lover. At his favorite ice cream shop, The Big Cone, you notice the lights are out for the letter E.

That evening, you return home to four dead plants. You get in a fight with your roommate. You tell her it is not healthy to repeat these types of patterns and that she is displaying symptoms of neurosis. You tell her that she needs to find new interests, other things to occupy her time, and decorate the apartment with something, anything else. She tells you it is her apartment too and that she can do as she pleases. She says you are being ridiculous and that they are only plants. You can't believe the way she is acting and think she must see that she is only bringing these plants home to die. If she truly can't, then you are certain you are right, and your roommate must be undeniably and completely insane.

One day, when you are walking to meet the last date of your project, you will see a stranger on the street and think it's your ex-lover again. But this time it is him. He looks at you quickly and then back again, confirming you are a person he has been acquainted with before. You will simply stare. He crosses the street to get to you. For a moment you imagine a car hitting him and his body being thrown like a puppet into the busy street.

When he makes it across safely, you think of running away or pretending you are not you. He looks the same, except he also has a new haircut. He asks how you are and you tell him you have been good, great actually. He says that he got a new job and started bowling. You tell him you learned pig Latin and how to juggle, and that you now collect plants. He seems impressed by this. He tells you he is running late and that he has to go. You say that it is fine, and you were just on your way to meet your date. He will say something like, "Oh" or "Don't let me keep you," and you will walk away while waving goodbye to him. On your way to meet William Henry Harrison, you will feel a sense of anticipation, of urgency to get to the restaurant. After all, he could very well be the one.

## Shrinking Space

It was a Wednesday morning when Eve first noticed her husband was shrinking. There was nothing out of the ordinary about the morning really, the two woke around their usual time, with Richard's alarm ringing promptly at seven.

They lay side by side together on the same mattress, in the same house they had lived in for five years. Richard rolled over and put his arm across Evelyn.

When Richard woke at seven every morning, he liked to be the one to wake his wife. Eve, however, had usually been awake for some time already, as her side of the bed was closest to the window. She enjoyed the way the sun shone in the morning, waking her gently, giving her a few calm moments to herself before the day began.

Eve felt Richard's warm breath on her neck. "Wake up," he shook her. "Be sure not to burn my eggs this morning like you did yesterday." For years now, Eve had been making him the same breakfast of two eggs scrambled, and one slice of whole-wheat toast with just a spread of grape jam.

She listened while he got up from the bed and made his way to the bathroom. The door shut with a click of the lock and Eve sunk into their mattress. When she and Richard first picked out their mattress, Richard insisted they get one that was extra firm because of how his lower back tended to act up. Now, she could hardly tell the mattress had ever once been firm. She seemed to sink into it so much that it might envelop her entire body, close right in on her, like a grave.

In the room next door, their five-year-old son, Nate, was lying awake in bed waiting for his mother. He laid in bed staring up at the glow-in-the-dark sticky stars and planets spread all over his ceiling.

Nate was the kind of child that didn't need much to make him happy. To Eve, he was the kind of child that radiated happiness. He had bright, blond curls and stunning, white crooked teeth. He had said that he wanted to be an astronaut when he grew up. After his father had told him that being an astronaut was not a real goal, not something he would probably ever do, Nate asked his mother to help him make his room look like it was space, just in case he didn't ever get there. And so his mother placed sticky stars and planets up on his ceiling so he could always fall asleep among his dreams. When Eve went into Nate's bedroom to wake him Wednesday morning, she found him awake already, staring up into his own galaxy.

They dressed and went down for breakfast where Eve found her husband struggling to retrieve a mug from the shelf in the kitchen. Looking at her husband, Eve felt there was something different about him. Richard was always an average-sized man. He was slim, but with defined muscles, with brown curls and bottle-green eyes. Although he now seemed to have lost close to four inches of height overnight. She stood next to him and reached the coffee mug with ease. In handing it to him, she found that he was now shorter than her.

Richard also seemed to notice this change and said, "It's those damn tall shoes you wear for work. I wish you would just wear normal shoes."

Eve's shoes for work barely had any heel at all, as her job was very demanding. She worked with preschool-age children all day, in a school about ten minutes from their home.

When she and Richard had first moved to Hudson to escape the busyness of New York City, she had not liked it at all. She loved the days she could spend reading in all the stores and coffee shops tucked neatly into the hectic streets of the city. She felt she could breathe there, among all that other chaos around her. But there in Hudson, with so much space around them, she felt only the chaos inside and feared it had become all-consuming.

"The city is no place for a child," Richard said. Eve had told Richard she did not want children, but three years into their marriage he gave her an ultimatum: a child or he would leave her.

"You're almost thirty-five already, and soon no one else will want you," he had said.

The next day, Eve found her husband sitting at the kitchen table, with his legs swinging back and forth. He had shrunk again, to half the size of the day before.

She heard Nate's footsteps on the stairs and watched his blond curls bounce up and down on his head as he skipped into the kitchen. He stopped short at the sight of his father.

"Daddy's a little boy!" Nate yelled, pointing at his father.

"It's that damn mattress," Richard said. "My back has been bothering me."

"We have to go to the doctor," Eve said.

"No doctors!" he yelled.

Eve thought it better that Richard stay in the house, so he didn't scare anyone who may see him like this. She went to work and dropped Nate at school, hoping her husband would be feeling better by the time she returned home.

"Richard!" she said when she got home. She searched the living room, their bedroom, the bathroom, and the kitchen where she had left him swinging his legs earlier that same morning.

She swore she could hear him calling her name, but she searched and searched and could not find her husband anywhere. She stopped and listened as closely as she could to the faint sound of her husband. She traced the sound into their bedroom where she found her husband in the middle of their bed jumping up and down.

She screamed out in shock at the sight of him. While she had been gone during the day, Richard had shrunk again, down to nearly the size of a pen. He was flailing his arms and legs and seemed to be shouting out but she could not hear a word he was saying.

She bent her head down and tilted her ear towards his tiny body.

"Pick me up!" he was saying.

She lifted her husband's body into the palm of her hand.

"Watch my back!" he yelled.

She held him at eye level and he stood in the middle of her palm with his hands on his hips. He shuffled around a bit in her palm, leaving her with a tickling sensation.

"You really ought to moisturize more. It's a bit rough up here," he said.

"What happened?" Eve said.

"Nothing. I'm feeling just fine," he said.

Eve heard the sound of the school bus pulling onto their street and tossed her husband back onto the bed.

"Hey! Careful!" he shouted, though he was no longer audible to Eve without being so close to her ear.

"Nate can't see you this way," she shouted at him.

She opened up the top drawer of their dresser that was lined with pairs of Richard's socks, now twice his size. She picked him up off the bed and dropped him into the drawer.

"Where's daddy?" Nate asked while eating a piece of toast with peanut butter and banana. He was sitting at the kitchen table, swinging his legs back and forth.

"Oh, he's fine. He had to go to the doctor for his back," said Eve.

The next day Richard demanded to be carried around by Eve.

"Put me in your purse. You won't even know I'm there," he said.

And so she did. She carried him around with her, hearing the squeaks that had become his voice and feeling his pinch in her palm when she picked him up to listen.

For days Eve convinced Nate that Daddy was away at the doctors and would be back soon. Eve could not decide what to do about her husband. Now that he was too small to do anything on his own, he demanded she bring him everywhere with her.

She found it difficult to do things she normally could with ease or with enjoyment, such as going to the grocery store or working with the children at school during the day.

At work, he wanted to be carried around in the pocket of her blouse, so he could talk to her throughout the day.

"This job is so easy," he said. "I could do this."

At the grocery store, he tried to climb out of her shirt pocket and onto her, desperately trying to talk into her ear. He scratched and bit at her chest. She thought about putting him in with the grapes but didn't want to risk anyone seeing him through the clear packaging. She thought about putting him in with the bread, but didn't want him to climb out of the bag. Finally, she decided to plop him into her purse.

Eve couldn't find a moment to herself, not even when she went to the bathroom. She asked Richard to have that time to herself, for her own privacy.

"You're being too sensitive," he said. "I am your husband."

And even when Nate's school announced they would be going to the Museum of Natural History for a field trip, he wanted to be placed in her purse and go along.

In the museum, Nate was quickly drawn to the galaxies exhibit. She watched her son scan the planets, carefully examining each one with his deep brown eyes.

In doing this she felt a rustling around in her purse.

Her husband was making his way up the inside of her purse and out the zipper. He was shimmying up the strap trying to get to her. Before she could stop him, he had grabbed hold of her sweater and was climbing up her shoulder. He latched onto her earlobe, pulling it tightly towards him and scratching her with his fingernails.

"He won't ever become an astronaut," he growled. Eve flicked at her ear and watched her husband lose his balance on her shoulder and fall back into her purse among a wad of tissues.

Eve watched Nate spin in circles while looking up at the hanging exhibits around them with the wonder she hoped would never leave him. She had never seen him so happy. She imagined he would one day become an astronaut and would travel to far, faraway places where the people were as happy as he was right now, and maybe one day he would even take her with him.

In the museum gift shop, Nate quickly located a rocket ship.

"It can be set off with a match," an employee said. "But it's not a toy."

"Please, please, please," said Nate.

Eve agreed to buy the rocket ship for Nate and while leaving the store felt a sharp pain in her rib cage. Her husband was using the tweezers from her purse to jab at her. She grabbed him out of her purse, opened the little door on the front of the rocket ship she had bought for Nate, and shoved her husband inside. In closing the door, she felt a sense of peace.

On the way home from the store, the winter air finally broke for the season and the sun felt of spring warmth. Eve shed her jacket and scarf like a heavy burden and found her son doing the same.

When they returned home, Nate pleaded with his mother to set off the rocket in the front yard with him.

"Okay," she said. "But, remember it's not a toy."

The two set the rocket up on its stand, pointing straight up to space, and Eve went inside to retrieve a box of matches.

She came back outside to see Nate bouncing up and down with excitement. She told him to stand back and lit the end of the string. They watched in anticipation for the rocket to launch, and only as the flame reached the end of the string did Eve remember placing her husband's tiny body inside. They watched the rocket shoot up with a final PING into the sky and then burst into tiny, unrecognizable pieces.

# Finding the Right Pet

Your mother recommends a fish while trying to unscramble the word "dismal" in the newspaper Saturday morning. Remember how your third-grade teacher, Ms. Riley, had a betta fish last year, and your whole class decided to name it Dennis but you wanted to name it Nemo.

Ask to go to the pet store right now, this second if possible, but your mother sips the coffee from her Rainforest Café mug she bought from Disney in 2006 and says, "Let me finish this."

At the pet store, a woman named Kristi, who has purple hair and a tattoo on her left wrist that says, "Find what you love and let it kill you" with the final letter wrapped up into a heart, brings you over to the betta fish. Remember the time you asked your mother if you could get a tattoo, and she told you that yes, you could, but not until you were an adult and had moved out. Remember how this made you furious and how you packed up your baby doll, blanky, blue backpack filled with chocolate chip chewy granola bars, and walked out the front door, declaring, "I am an adult and I am moving out."

While looking at the betta fish case, a small blue one, with a tint of purple near its eyes, the same shade as Kristi's hair, captures your attention. Kristi says she likes that one very much and asks what you are going to name it.

"Nemo!" you say, yelling at Kristi.

"Honey! Volume," your mother says, instantly turning you down, just as she did the late-night *Law and Order* episode that continued to play on the television last night after your father passed out.

Kristi's eyebrows are scrunched together, and she asks why you would name a betta fish Nemo when Nemo was a clownfish. You will not understand what this means. Begin to tell her about Ms. Riley and Dennis and those kids who all decided to name him the same thing. Your mother cuts you off to ask about fishbowls.

That evening, your father returns home at seven o'clock to find that your mother has moved his favorite chair slightly to the left to make room for the bookcase that now holds Nemo's bowl. He asks where she gets off moving his things, and when she tells him that he cannot tell her where to place her own goddamn furniture, he will burst into a fit of laughter.

Your father always laughs like he means it. He laughs as if he is the only one left in the world and no one would ever hear. Throwing his head back in a fit of laughter, with his slick black hair following behind, he shakes the room.

Nemo dies Monday morning while you are in school.

In the afternoon, right after science and just before lunchtime, receive your new Spanish vocabulary words for the week. Be sure to listen when señora tells you this is a tough list this week and that we must use the correct articles to indicate the gender of the word. For example: *el papa* (pope) versus *la papa* (potato).

"Please pay attention to the articles of the nouns, niños," she says. "Words can have many meanings."

Meanwhile, your mother frantically searches for a way to spare your heartbreak and will discover online that she can freeze Nemo and bring him back to the store to return him for a new fish for free (receipt from date of purchase necessary).

After freezing and returning five dead Nemos, your mother is no longer able to find a blue betta fish, and you will begin to get suspicious. "Yes, fish do change colors," your mother says. "They are like your mood necklace."

Search for the tiny pamphlet that came along with your dolphin mood necklace and find it stuffed in the kitchen junk drawer underneath the hammer and multi-color paper clips. Look on the color wheel for the color blue. Discover that blue most often means: "relaxed, at ease, calm, lovable."

Run back to the bookcase next to your father's chair to decipher the exact current color of your fish. Find that Nemo looks like an orange-red, leaning more towards red. He reminds you of the leaves that blow onto your driveway from your neighbor's big tree in the fall. Open your pamphlet to find that the color red most often means: "anxious, angered, alarmed, fearful."

Several days later, overhear your father call your home a "fish hospice." Ask your mother what a hospice is.

"It makes your food spicy," she says.

Recall the time you accidentally ate a very hot pepper off the cheese and cracker plate at your cousin's birthday party.

"I don't think I would like hospice," you will declare.

At the dinner table, over a steaming hot plate of pepper and olive oil spaghetti, your father suggests getting a frog.

Kristi shows you and your mother the pet store's grand selection of two frogs. She brings you over to the green, dumpy, tree frog. He is slimy and sticky and does nothing at all. Fall in love with him immediately.

As she rings up your purchase, Kristi informs you and your mother that Dumpy, as you have named him, eats only live crickets. She walks you over to a large case containing crickets and cardboard. The crickets are climbing on the cardboard, all the way to the top, and attempting to jump out of the shut glass. They hit the top of the case and fall back to the bottom only to begin again.

Your mother attempts to disappear into thin air as she watches Kristi scoop the crickets into a small container for you to take home.

Dumpy lives for a long time, too long. You feed him live crickets each night, and you wake up at 2 a.m. to the sound of a loose cricket in the house that has escaped from its imminent death by Dumpy's sticky tongue.

One night, when your mother finds several live crickets on the bathroom counter, you surrender Dumpy to your fifth-grade science teacher, Mr. Miller, as a class pet because your mother cannot take it anymore. Your class loves Dumpy, and watching his long tongue catch the live crickets is the highlight of the classroom activities for exactly two months. After that, your class forgets about

Dumpy as he says and does nothing.

Come back after Christmas break to find that Dumpy is gone. Ask where he is. Mr. Miller will tell you calmly that he has died of starvation. Be shocked. Cry. Blame Nolan, the boy who sits next to the window in your class and draws pictures of stick figures with big boobs.

Mr. Miller tells the class not to be upset, and that he has a surprise for you all. He walks behind his desk to retrieve something.

He lifts up a fishbowl and places it on his desk. Stare at the blue betta fish as it swims in a small circle and then stops to look back at you.

"What should we name him?" Mr. Miller asks.

Do not wince or argue when the class decides to name him Fred.

## Fat Lady

Someone once asked me, "When did you find the time to eat all that food?" Well, it was easy. I'll tell you. I worked as a secretary at an otolaryngology office, more commonly known as the ear, nose, and throat doctor. I didn't do much besides check people in, check people out, look up insurance, and enter other information like that into the computer. Oh, and I ate. Me and the other ladies in the office took turns bringing in baked goods, so I always had a mid-morning and mid-afternoon snack. Janet baked the best snickerdoodle cookies and I was known for my peanut butter cookies. But that was all coming to an end.

My primary doctor of ten years, Dr. Gray, told me I was 260 pounds and needed to lose weight before it started to put too much stress on my heart. "Heart problems do run in your family," he reminded me.

My grandmother died of a massive heart attack at age sixty-two. It was very sudden. But she was almost 400 pounds and was warned many times by her doctors as well.

"Your grandmother, she died of a heart attack I believe?" Dr. Gray asked passively while staring at his chart.

"Yes," I said. "She died at sixty-two."

"Well, you've got a good twenty-five years yet till you hit the sixty mark, but let's get on this now."

So I went on a liquid diet, drinking only fruits, veggies, and a bit of protein powder. Something like a cleanse. It was terrible. I still have flashbacks of the hunger pains I would wake up to at three o'clock in the morning. I was never big into vegetables, but I couldn't wait until my next smoothie throughout the day. Three-quarters of my usual calories were cut out of my diet. Certainly, this wasn't what my doctor had in mind when he told me to "eat better," but I thought if I was going to do it, I might as well go all the way.

The weight started dropping quickly. Weeks were flying by, and I was sticking to my diet. I was also exercising. I was walking every morning before work for two hours. The pounds were coming off. People started noticing. Janet in the office couldn't understand why I wouldn't eat her snickerdoodle cookies anymore. For her, this was the biggest tragedy.

I could hardly believe how loose my clothes were beginning to feel. It was like a miracle. But I wasn't done yet, and I was still overweight. I had to start incorporating other foods into my diet, like lean proteins. I alternated cooked fish and grilled chicken with rice for my dinner each night.

The woman at the counter in the grocery store was

starting to recognize me, and we would always say hello to each other. But my trips to the grocery store only reminded me of the weight I still had to lose. All the aisles that I usually would visit only stood to haunt me.

One Sunday, I was making my way over to the green peppers when I accidentally bumped into a young man by the tomatoes. He was wearing a black sleeveless top and camouflage cargo shorts. He looked annoyed the moment I hit him, and as he opened his mouth to yell at me, I noticed a piercing through his tongue.

"Watch it, fat lady," he said. He grabbed three large tomatoes and then walked around me. He reminded me of a young boy that had been in my middle school English class. The boy had bright red hair and ugly teeth with braces that looked like they may fall out any minute. He had nicknamed me Oreo because that's what I had in my lunch pack every day.

"You're rounder than an Oreo," he said, and that nickname stuck. Throughout middle school and high school, I was Oreo.

But my diet did finally pay off. After several long and exhausting months, I had lost one hundred pounds. I never thought the day would come that I would say I had lost weight, let alone one hundred pounds.

I noticed I was treated differently. People were polite to me when I dropped the weight. Men held doors for me, offered to carry my chicken and fish out of the grocery store to my car, and even people at work treated me differently.

One of the doctors at my job was a real jerk, Dr. Arpin. His family was French. Dr. Arpin was a good-looking man, and he knew it. Slick hair and a neat beard, toned arms. A sharp dresser too, with his nice navy suit under his medical coat. He would often stir up trouble between the nurses, especially the new ones when they would discover that he had slept with more than one of them.

It was a Friday, and he had just finished telling a patient that the lump on the back of her tonsils was cancerous and she would need radiation therapy. She was softly crying in room number four when he came out of the room, plopped her papers onto my desk and announced, "There's only two more hours left until the weekend." Janet spun around briefly in her chair to roll her eyes.

I could still feel him standing next to me. His presence was like a fruit fly. I could feel it, but I didn't want to look because then I would be forced to deal with it.

"Is there something I can help you with, doctor?" I asked him, finally turning to meet his eyes.

"I was just thinking," he continued, "we're going to have to cut your pay in half because you've lost a whole person," he said.

Janet gasped. "What is wrong with you!" she practically screamed at him.

"Oh, come on," Dr. Arpin said. "I'm just kidding."

"Right," I said, reassuring him with a smile.

I truly wasn't so much upset by what Dr. Arpin said, but struck by the thought that I had in fact lost a whole person. I had shed the weight of another human being. The thought consumed my mind the rest of the day, and I began to obsess over it.

That same night, I had a dream that me and a skinnier, maybe hundred-pound version of myself were floating out in the middle of the ocean. All we had to survive was this small plank that was big enough for only one of us, and we kept struggling and fighting one another for that spot. It was much like a *Titanic* situation, although neither one of us were willing to play the role of Jack and die so the other could live. Also, in my dream at least, there really was only room for one of us on the plank. I won in the end, drowning my hundred-pound self and watching her drift down to the bottom of the ocean.

I woke the next morning covered in sweat and breathing heavily. I felt that I had killed some version of myself unintentionally. I rose and went for my usual two-hour morning walk. Along the way, I started to feel much calmer, reminding myself it was only a dream, and that dreams help us process change in our lives. I had lost one hundred pounds for god's sake! I should be damn proud. I was down to 160 pounds, lower than I could ever remember being in my adulthood.

By the end of the walk, I was feeling much better, walking with an air of confidence in my step. But when I returned to my house, I found the hundred-pound version of myself sitting on the steps of my front porch. The same version of myself that I had seen, and killed, just the night before in my dream.

I screamed. I thought I must be still dreaming. It wasn't real. Couldn't be. But it was. She had the same short, pin-straight blonde hair that I've always hated all my life and unsuccessfully tried to curl, the same big ears that my mother used to say meant that I was a really good listener, and that puzzle piece shaped birthmark on the right side of her neck. I ran past my hundred-pound self, through my front door, slammed it shut behind me, and locked it firmly.

On Monday, I tried explaining to Janet what happened while she stared at the egg on the side of my head. She assured me it was probably just my body adjusting to losing so much weight so quickly, but she suggested maybe I should go talk to someone.

She gave me the number of a woman that she had gone to who specialized in anxiety and obsessive thoughts. Janet had gone to see her when her oldest dog, one of her six Dalmatians, died from being hit by a garbage truck when she forgot to close her gate.

I thought of my sister, Jean, only for a moment. I had not thought of her in some time, too long of a time. She was diagnosed with lymphoma at six years old, and it was a slow, painful death for her. She was two years older than me, and I don't really remember much about her, but I do remember my parents during that time. They were both so serious and sad, hurrying about the house and the hospital rooms. I was eight years old when she finally did die. At the end, she looked as if she could have been my younger sister by several more years, with her skin collapsing into her tiny bones, and the skin around her eyes drooping like an old woman's. She was so small; I wasn't even allowed in her room. My parents fretted over her body like a prized piece of china glass.

I don't think my mother ever got over it. I moved away for work and we don't speak much anymore, mostly just our usual check-in during the holidays. I thought this was something I could discuss in therapy. This was the kind of thing people talked about, right? Childhood trauma. Janet told me she helped her with the trauma in her life. She explained to her that there is Capital T trauma and lowercase t trauma. I thought that my sister's death could definitely have been a Capital T trauma.

On the therapist's website, it said she had private and confidential sessions with her patients and no matter what situation her patients were in they were always treated with respect. I wondered what she would think of my situation. Seeing a hundred-pound version of myself in reality after killing that same version of myself in my dreams.

I thanked Janet for her recommendation and decided I would keep this therapist in the back of my mind in case I really needed her, but I felt like one episode did not constitute an immediate trip to a therapist. More weeks went by and I stayed steady around 160 pounds, every few days wandering into the 150 range, but usually right around 160, never higher.

I had gone back to a somewhat normal diet. Lots of protein still and grains. The seafood department at the grocery store all knew me now.

During one of my usual Sunday night trips to the grocery store, I placed my order with one of the workers at the counter. It was a small girl with her head down working the counter, and I didn't recognize her. She did not respond to me when I first said hello or even after I told her what I would like to order, but instead, she slowly looked up at me.

I saw her seafood department hat rising as she lifted her head to show her face. Those ears were unmistakable, and as her hair fell down her back, I saw the birthmark on her neck.

"You cannot get rid of me," she said.

It was me again. Well not me, but the hundred-pound version. I screamed out, just like I had on my front porch, and turned to run from her and the fish she had somehow reached out to give me in the midst of everything. As I did, I ran into the tank full of lobsters and fell on top of them. They all came tumbling out, crawling over me as best they could with the rubber bands around their claws. The workers behind the counter scrambled to pick them up off of me.

I smelled like fish for the next two weeks. I thought it best to give the therapist a call. She was very interested when speaking with me on the phone. I gave her a brief summary of my situation. I told her I had recently lost a great amount of weight and was having some obsessive thoughts about the weight I had lost.

"Not a problem at all!" she said. She seemed up for the challenge, though she didn't know all the true details yet.

"How's Thursday afternoon?" she asked.

In my first session with Jo (she informed that her real name was Joanna though she preferred to be called Jo in both the personal and professional setting), I felt that I had made a very big mistake. She spoke a great deal about my weight loss, why I decided to do it, and how I felt now. She wanted to know if I had always been overweight, if others in my family were, etc. I was struggling to find the words to tell her what was really going on. When our hour was up, she asked me if I would like to schedule another session for the same time the following week. I agreed, thinking I should give it another chance, just as I had for Dr. Gray. After all, if it weren't for him, I wouldn't have lost the weight in the first place.

That week I avoided public places as much as I could out of fear of seeing myself. I only left the house for work and then came straight home at the end of the day. I lived off the canned soups I had stocked up on months ago and didn't dare return to that grocery store—to the scene of the crime.

By the time Thursday came around again, I had lost another three pounds, most likely due to stress and from eating tomato or cream of mushroom soup for all three meals.

At our second session, Jo was wearing a floral shirt and a hot pink skirt, both of which felt entirely inappropriate for my current state of mind. I thought if I was going to be honest with Jo, now was the time to do it.

I started my story from the beginning. I told her about the snickerdoodle cookies, the smoothies, the dream, the lobsters, and of course, the hundred-pound version sightings. When I finished, I felt that I had just ran several miles which I had never actually done. I was out of breath, sweating, and crying.

Jo was sitting very still, not saying a word. I thought it best to give her a moment to process all that I had just told her. She began nodding her head slowly and jotted something down in her notepad. She then dropped her notepad and pen to the ground suddenly, almost throwing it across the floor at my feet.

There was only one thing written on the entire sheet of white paper. It said, "You can't get rid of me." I picked up the notebook and looked to Jo, but Jo was no longer herself. I was staring again at the hundred-pound version of myself.

As I was running out of the office, I wondered if I could

get my money back for our two sessions as clearly, I was not meeting with a therapist after all. I thought maybe I had been scammed by myself.

That night I had soup again for dinner. The whole can of soup was about 320 calories, which would bring my calorie count for the day to 1,600. I remembered when I used to eat a cheeseburger and fries as an afternoon snack that was 1,100 calories alone, not counting the extra fries I always requested.

I slept and dreamt of my hundred-pound self. This time, I did not kill her; I was watching her from afar, almost stalking her. I watched her eating, marveling at how she seemed to be satisfied after eating only two scrambled eggs and a piece of toast with jam for her breakfast. Her skinny bones reminded me of twigs on the ground, they were so delicate. She looked so fragile in my dream, and I reached out to touch her bones, but when I did, she disintegrated right in front of me and fell to the ground.

I was running out of soup. I knew I had to go back to the grocery store and I didn't want to go to a new one because I already knew where everything was in the old one, and I could get in and out of there quickly. I decided to go.

I slowly made my way to the back of the store where the seafood counter was. I was afraid to see what they did with the lobster case. I wondered if it would even still be there. By now I'm sure most of the employees would know some crazy woman had crashed into the lobsters and knocked them over.

I hovered at the end of the cracker and cereal aisle to get a peek at the seafood counter. I saw all the usual workers and noticed the lobster case had been replaced with new, thicker glass and a fresh set of lobsters. I turned down the next aisle, giving myself another moment before taking on the task of ordering my fish. It was the cookies and snack aisle, completely empty except for one small girl on the left side of the aisle, holding two boxes of what looked like snickerdoodle and peanut butter cookies. She didn't have a cart with her, no purse, and she was shaking. I watched her taking the cookies out of their boxes one by one, alternating between the two kinds, and shoving them into her mouth.

"Excuse me," I said, walking closer to her. "Excuse me, are you alright?"

She did not acknowledge that I was speaking to her, and I placed my hand on her shoulder and asked again if she was alright. But before she turned towards me, with a half-eaten cookie in her mouth, I saw the puzzle piece birthmark on the side of her neck, and I knew that it was me.

She looked so small, thin, those one hundred pounds of her body looking like nothing at all. I thought the cookies might instead swallow her whole. I felt disgusted that she was eating this way. This certainly was not the same, delicate girl from my dream who ate so little, although she did have the same tiny bones, and wrists so small that the brown hair tie on her left wrist struggled to stay on.

I slapped the boxes out of her hands.

"No more!" I yelled. "Look how far you've come!"

But instead of slapping the boxes out of her hand, I felt

the weight of the snickerdoodle and peanut butter cookie boxes in my own hands. I felt the crumbs between my teeth and the sharp, sweet taste of sugar on my tongue.

I was shoving cookies into my mouth, one by one, alternating between the two kinds.

I was no longer in control of myself. I couldn't stop. I felt all my hard work over the past months wasting away in the boxes of cookies. I couldn't even taste anymore, but I knew that I had to keep going.

I was down to the last snickerdoodle cookie, so consumed with them that I didn't notice my hundred-pound self was gone. I ate the last cookie, wiped the crumbs from my lips, and dropped the box to the ground.

# Dead to Me

For days, weeks, months, I had imagined that you were dead. I pictured it, saw you buried in the ground with no casket, naked in the dirt, with insects crawling all around you. I imagined awful things happening to you, things so terrible and ridiculous that they almost made me laugh. I imagined you died by some nasty infection that gave you a high fever and eventually killed you. I imagined you finally got into a car crash while driving home drunk from the bar, crashing head-on into the big oak tree right before the highway, and flying through the windshield, decapitating yourself with a branch. I admit that these were awful things to think of. They were thoughts out of anger. And I only thought of these things when I was thinking of you the least.

I would even tell people when they asked how I was doing, how I was "recovering," that I didn't think of you at all, hardly gave you a moment of my precious time, even said that you were dead to me.

But the worst part was that you were alive, and I knew this. You were still out there, breathing, going on, and living. Your bright blue eyes, dirty blond hair, and toned muscles that weren't always put to the best use. I even imagined that you were happy. Maybe starting something new. I imagined these things when thinking of you the most.

I would obsessively search for clues in our past and try to figure out where it all could have gone wrong. I went back through the years, photos, trying to map out each weekend, each night spent together and figure out where I had lost you. Other days I tried to pinpoint where I even had you to begin with.

There were days when I would try and forget you altogether. I rented a U-Haul, went through our house and collected all of your things, anything that reminded me of you. I collected the photos of us, the paintings you got from China, that stupid glass globe you insisted on having in the living room, and packed it all up in the truck. It wasn't until I was sitting in the driver's seat that I realized I had nowhere to go.

Other days, you were once again the man I had married, and I decided that what happened between us was nothing but a terrible dream. You were mowing the lawn or drinking a beer on the front porch. I was writing or out on a run and we still spent every evening together, making dinner like we always did, tacos or pasta, just waiting for the night to come and the day to be over so we could finally be alone together. The only two people in the world.

So it was when I got the call exactly one year, six

months and two days after I left you that you actually had died, I thought it must be a joke.

"Like really dead?" I asked on the phone.

It was your mother that called me, and I hadn't heard from her in exactly one year, two months and ten days since she sent me a text that would go unanswered asking, "How are you?"

I had thought of changing my phone number many times before for this reason exactly, so that the people, ghosts really, of that time in my life, of the time of you, didn't come seeping back through the cracks undetected. But I was there once again, answering her call.

She was sobbing uncontrollably, so much so that I almost didn't hear when she said that you had killed yourself.

I was unsure of how to respond. I always thought you to be too bold or prideful to do something like that. But she told me that you had done it and that there was just a sticky note left behind on the counter of your apartment with the name of a motel.

People rarely left our town, not because Hudson was all that great, but especially not during the brutal winter New York was having that year—I didn't think people even wanted to leave their homes. But later that day, as I read the address for the motel off Google, I saw that it was just a couple miles outside of town.

Your mother said they found you in the bathtub; they being the cleaning ladies. You had done it, slit your wrists with some disposable razor from the dollar store down the street and bled out alone—just like that.

I wanted to feel better. That's what I thought I would feel. My usual daydreams of your death brought some kind of relief, but instead I felt worse.

It was two months after I learned of your death that I started staying at the motel. Just one night on the weekend, nothing crazy. It was cheap and I would request a different room every time, except for number four. I know that's where you did it. By now it was cleaned out and the people who stayed there had no idea that some man had slit his wrists in the bathtub. But I bet that if they looked close enough, they might still be able to find a drop of your blood caked in the tile on the bathroom floor.

When I got my assigned room for the night, I would slip the key into the lock carefully, as if I might disturb someone already inside, and feel my heart in my stomach. I searched for clues in the room. The television remote, the bedspread, the napkins on the desk. I thought about the relationship you and the motel had before you did it. I thought about how you felt. But there was never anything there for me to discover or understand. No clue, no answer. Just another cheap, ugly, lonely room.

Each Saturday night I would order in at the Blue Fish Motel and watch terrible television: reruns of *Law and Order*, the *Maury Show*, anything I could while eating takeout Chinese food or pizza.

It was the fifth Saturday night that I was staying at the motel when your mother called me again.

"Hello?" I said, answering the phone with hot and sour soup dribbling down my chin. She asked me to meet her for dinner at an Italian restaurant we used to go to back when you were alive. More importantly, back when you and I were together. I said I would meet her in an hour.

Outside of the motel, I could hear people. I peeked out of the closed blinds to see a girl about three years old and another maybe a year old sitting on a blanket with a woman nearby. The woman looked to be around my age, maybe thirty, with long brown hair like I used to have before I cut it off at my shoulders.

I had been pregnant once. I was twelve weeks the night I lost the baby and you. Sometimes I still blame your death on the drinking and other times I wonder if you would have done it even if you were sober and it wasn't late at night but instead in the middle of the afternoon.

I had never really wanted children, but you said this was what people did and I would do it or you would leave. So I got pregnant. But knowing I was didn't stop the arguing and it didn't stop your anger.

The idea of having something of my own carried me for a while. But it didn't last long. And now, after everything, it's the things that almost were that seem to still matter the most to me. My mind makes up for the difference in what could have been. I used to imagine lives for you and me and the baby, good lives, back when we were almost happy. But that was all before. And after, I only imagined you were dead until eventually, you were.

When I got to the restaurant, your mom was already there wearing a raggedy V-neck shirt and jean capris like she always did. She reminded me of a penguin when she walked, not meaning to limp, but always having a problem with her left knee that she never did anything about.

"Karla!" she said and reached out to hug me. Her embrace was uncomfortable and while I let her hold me for a moment, I tried to imagine the last time I had hugged or even touched anyone else.

For dinner she ordered chicken parmesan and ate exactly half of what was on her plate.

"Can't eat like I used to!" she said. She told me about the kids at her job and asked how I was liking work. I had been an assistant at a law firm for five years and had to take some time off after all that happened, but had been back for a few months. I told her everything was fine. Each time I finished speaking she would wait a few seconds longer, as if there was something else I was meant to say.

"And," she started, "you're all healed up?"

I thought about telling your mother that you had already been dead to me for over a year now and all the ways you had already died were much worse than how you actually did. I thought about telling her of the insects, the car crash, the decapitation, but in the end I didn't.

For the first time in weeks, I lifted my hand to my scalp to feel for the scar.

"Yes. All healed up," I said.

She nodded and sipped at her wine. This was something new. She never drank. You and your father drank plenty, maybe enough for both me and your mother. But now at dinner she already had two glasses of wine.

"I did believe you, you know," she said, hiding partially behind her glass.

I could feel myself warming. I sweat awfully whenever I felt uncomfortable. My cheeks would redden and I could feel the perspiration under my arms. I brought the back of my hand up to my cheek and felt its suffocating warmth. If this had been a few months ago, I probably would have walked right out of the restaurant. Maybe I would have yelled at your mother, or I may not have even come to the restaurant at all. But some things are excused in grief.

"Thank you," I said. At the time, I wasn't sure anyone believed me, but I quickly realized most everyone already knew.

The night I lost you and the baby was the same night I almost died. I had never imagined a death for myself in the same way that I had started imagining your death after I left you.

I usually knew better than to even be awake when you came home drunk. You were awful when you drank and nobody, including me, ever had the guts to tell you. I really didn't even mean to be awake, but it was around eleven and my younger sister had called. She just got back from a trip abroad in Italy. Well, you didn't know who I was talking to on the phone and when you came storming into the house, barely walking straight, you said, "You're a fucking slut."

I really was standing too close to the stairs, and I never liked the way they were next to the kitchen—a real hazard. When you were hitting me you probably felt the suffocating warmth of my face as I desperately tried to explain to you that it was only my sister, but I was already falling.

They had to stitch my scalp back together and the concussion was so bad that for weeks I was slurring my words. My sister wouldn't let you into my room at the hospital. You sat out in the waiting room for six days. I don't know how you did it. It was when the nurse finally came in to tell me I had lost the baby too that she asked me how it was I actually fell down the stairs so hard. You were arrested on your seventh day in the waiting room. You spent a year in prison and were finally on probation when you killed yourself.

"He was my son," your mother said. "I really didn't think he was that bad."

The "almosts" were filled in for me with what came after. People told me how sorry they were, how they couldn't believe it. But after you really died, nobody said they were sorry for that. Nobody really said anything to me about it besides your mother.

I saw you alive a week after having dinner with her. You looked just like you, except two inches shorter and wearing a yellow striped shirt you never would have worn. You looked in my direction and I realized that he wasn't you. I wanted to know how much longer I would have to keep these pieces of you. These pieces of you in life and in death. How much longer? How much longer would it be until your mother moved on? Until she stopped calling, asking how I was, though she once bought baby clothes and had given us money, and helped me buy my wedding dress? If you had already died twice to me now and I was still seeing you, would I ever stop?

I often think about our last day together. Not the day of the stairs and the hospital and the phone call, but our real last day together. The day before it all. It was a Friday. We both had off of work, and we had walked in the park for three hours. We gave names to birds we would never see again. You carried me across the street to our car when I was absolutely exhausted from walking. I think I knew in so many ways that day. Maybe you even told me in your own way that there was a dying coming. The way you decided to cook for us that night, the way you went to bed an hour later than usual, even the way you kissed me on my forehead. I think I knew all along.

# Eyes Shut

It happened the year Thanksgiving was held at her in-laws. Estelle never did much like Perry and Laurie, but they were her husband's side of the family and she had come to accept them as best she could. It was something about the way they were to Jimmy, how he was always on edge around them.

Jimmy was thirteen, and he hated school and tried to tell his mother this, but Estelle told him it was all a part of growing up, and that he would have to learn to deal with it.

Jimmy was not an ordinary child. He was teased in school, though he was not teased for the normal things kids were usually made fun of for, like being too quiet or having braces, or chunky glasses that made their eyes pop. Jimmy was teased because he had a large head. His head was abnormally large, about twice the size of a normal child's head. In fact, his skull was twice the size for a normal boy his age.

Jimmy knew he was different. He knew he was different when the boys at school would ask if his head was going to explode, and he knew it when he had to go to the doctor for neck pain from carrying around the weight of his head. He especially knew it when his cousins, Jack and Matt, would imitate the weight of his head, walking around like Frankenstein, pretending they could not carry their own heads on their shoulders.

Estelle knew it too, and she knew how Jack and Matt felt about Jimmy, but she never thought they would go so far.

Estelle told Jimmy that his large head only made him special, not strange. "You have more brainpower," she said. "That's where you get your smarts from."

Jimmy was smart. He had the best grades in his class. He had already been taking high school math classes, and even those were easy for him. This only made the kids dislike him more and kids could be mean.

"It's only going to get worse for him next year," Estelle tried to warn her husband. She had worked as a science teacher in the high school before she quit when she was pregnant with Jimmy, and she knew what the kids would be like to him.

Her husband was a quiet man. He seemed to take nothing seriously and this bothered Estelle. His air of complete indifference made her furious.

The in-laws, however, were completely different from her husband. They were hyper, nosy, and bothered by everything. She could never understand how her husband, so quiet and steadfast, could tolerate their behavior. It seemed to her that being around them made him quieter, more certain that he was acting the correct way.

That Thanksgiving started off wrong when they arrived late, due to Jimmy not wanting to go.

"Why can't we have dinner together, just the three of us?" he pleaded. He seemed genuinely scared to go to his cousins' house, which made Estelle concerned.

"I guess we could," Estelle said, looking to her husband.

"I told them we would be there, and so we are going," he said, and that was the end of it. Jimmy then shut his eyes tight, like he had seen something he didn't want to.

This had become a habit of his, shutting his eyes tight. He did this whenever he felt threatened. Estelle was not sure where he had learned this from, but ever since elementary school, when his head started growing larger than the other kids, he started shutting his eyes. It became an immediate reaction for him. He seemed to believe that if he couldn't see what was going on, he couldn't hear it either. He could instead disappear inside himself.

The teasing and harassing was finally getting to him, at least that's what Estelle thought it must be. She had met with the principal on several occasions that year, especially after the bus incident.

Some of the boys on the bus had found a nail under their seat and thought it would be funny to shoot it with a rubber band at Jimmy's big head.

"The perfect target!" they had called him.

When the teasing started that day on the bus and they threatened to shoot the nail at him, he shut his eyes tight as he always did. The nail cut him right across his right eye. He needed four stitches and wouldn't open his eyes until his mother arrived at the hospital to pick him up. The doctors told her his eye was spared only because he shut them long before the boys shot the nail at his head.

Seeing Jimmy shut his eyes again on Thanksgiving only reminded Estelle of when he first started doing it, and she wanted nothing more than to protect him and shelter him like she did when he was younger. But he was older now, and his father was starting to lose patience with it.

"Here we go with this again," said his father, and walked out to the car.

"Darling, open your eyes," said Estelle. Jimmy slowly opened his eyes, one at a time, pleading with her not to make him go.

Perry and Laurie lived in a beautiful home in the Adirondack Mountains. Their home was at the bottom of a large hill, right next to the lake. They were an active family, doing lots of kayaking and swimming in the nice weather. They also loved to ski in the winter. The location could not have been more perfect for them.

But there was something about that day. Estelle wasn't exactly sure when she first felt it. Maybe it was when she stepped out of the car, or when she walked into their house, with the three dead deer heads hanging on the wall like trophies, or maybe even when she saw Jimmy's cousins snicker at him, and laugh as he walked through the door behind her. She would never be sure just when the moment was that she knew something awful would happen.

Her husband greeted his brother, Perry, with a big hug, and kissed Laurie on the cheek. The turkey was almost done. Estelle could smell it. They had brought a sweet potato casserole and green beans with sliced almonds and garlic, Jimmy's favorite.

The house was like a shrine to their sons. Several years older than Jimmy, the boys played sports at the high school. One was a sophomore basketball star and the other a junior football quarterback. Estelle learned of all their triumphs over dinner as she played with her sweet potatoes, creating a hole in the middle of them to make a gravy pond.

"I hear Jimmy is doing well in school also. Quite the student?" Laurie said. Laurie was a neat woman. Her outfit matched almost too perfectly with light shades of gray and pink. Her top flowed down to her capris at just the right height. Her body was decorated with all sorts of bracelets, necklaces, beads, and a pair of hoop earrings.

"Yes, he's doing great," said Estelle.

"More like quite the nerd," said the older of the two boys, Jack. He was tall, lean muscles, and long, black hair slicked down with gel. He looked like a football player. He was over six foot.

"Jack!" said Laurie, shooting him an angry look.

The other boy, Matt, snorted at the comment.

For dessert there was pumpkin pie and cherry tarts. Homemade of course, Laurie was great at baking. Jack and Matt both shoved down two mini tarts each while Jimmy picked at his slice of pie.

Estelle didn't often look to her husband for help when it came to Jimmy, as he didn't seem to mind one way or the other. But after what the boys had said, she looked right to him. Their eyes met briefly, his dark brown eyes darting away from hers. He was wearing long, tan khakis with an orange collar shirt and a navy V-neck sweater pulled over the top. He was a handsome man, and she suddenly wondered if he had ever been unfaithful to her. His dark eyes and blond curls must have attracted many of the women working in his law firm, and it occurred to Estelle then that she had never thought of it before. His entire appearance seemed to suggest that he had something important to say but was too afraid to say it, and Estelle knew not even the beautiful women with their long legs and pencil skirts could get it out of him.

"Why don't you boys go outside?" her husband suggested. His solution to the situation clearly to rid the adults of the boys.

"Oh, yes!" said Laurie. "There is a lovely view of the lake up on top of the hill. A bit of a walk, but the boys could show it to Jimmy!" Laurie was so upbeat and cheery all the time that Estelle couldn't help but not trust her.

Jimmy looked to his mother for her approval. He wanted to go, that was for sure. He wanted so much to be included in something, anything that the normal kids did.

"Go ahead. Just be careful," said Estelle.

The two older boys slid out of their chairs and headed for the door. The oldest, Jack, took the lead.

Laurie and Perry could drink. Estelle had two glasses of wine since she had been there and she could already feel a light buzz. Her husband was finishing his third, but both Perry and Laurie were halfway through their fifth glass and didn't seem to be affected by it at all.

This was how it always went at their gatherings, the few times they actually got together every several years.

There was a meal, some dessert, and then what

seemed to be the real treat for the adults—plenty of drinks.

Estelle preferred the red wine over the white. It felt smoother, calming the anxious feeling that hadn't left her since they pulled up to the house. Or was it when they first came in? She still wasn't sure.

She drank small sips at a time, never with the intention of getting drunk, but around her husband and in-laws, she could feel a kind of floating sensation, almost like a second-hand intoxication from watching them.

Perry and Laurie had a beautiful deck overlooking the water. It was cold out, the November air starting to warn of the winter to come. They all had coats on, but Estelle still felt a chill through all the layers she wore. The four of them sat outside, lounging in Adirondack chairs. They had brought their wine glasses and the bottles out with them onto the deck.

The boys started up the steep hill behind the house. They used pieces of debris that had fallen from the trees as walking sticks to aid their climb and avoid the rocks.

Jimmy was cold. All three boys were only wearing long-sleeved t-shirts. His cousins hadn't grabbed their jackets on the way out, so Jimmy hadn't either, something he knew his mother would have fussed over.

Jimmy's cousins seemed to be in a hurry, walking way ahead of him. He was struggling to keep up, his legs like sticks compared to his cousins. His shoulders were also hurting, which often happened when he did anything strenuous, having to carry the weight of his head, making it difficult for him to keep moving.

"Could you guys slow down?" he yelled out. They didn't even turn around, just kept on moving forward.

Jimmy could feel his teeth chattering. *Why hadn't he grabbed a jacket?* he silently scolded himself as his mother would.

What worried him more than the cold was the nausea he felt rising in his gut. He was getting nervous, and he knew what happened when he got nervous.

Laurie was definitely drunk. She was talking about how young her boys were the first time she realized that they would be great athletes when she burst into tears.

"Oh, I can just remember it. I knew they would be great," she said. "It goes by so fast!"

Estelle's husband handed Laurie his handkerchief from his pocket and rubbed her shoulder as if he truly felt empathetic towards her.

"I'm so sorry," said Laurie. "How rude of me."

"What do you mean?" asked Estelle.

"How unfair of me to talk about my sons like that as if you could possibly understand."

Estelle could feel the pressure inside her chest pushing on her like a weight she couldn't handle.

"What does that mean?" she snapped back at Laurie.

"Why don't we just drop it," said Estelle's husband.

Laurie had never liked Jimmy. Or maybe it was that she did like him, only in the sense that he made her and her sons feel more superior.

"I feel the same way about my son as well," said Estelle. The tension on the deck was unmistakable.

"Of course, of course," Laurie assured Estelle. Estelle felt it again then—that feeling. Something wasn't right. *Could it be the wine?* No, she was still only on her second glass.

It was in the air. She knew it. It was a similar anxiety, one that she thought she had felt many times before, but this time it was more intense, and suddenly she became certain of exactly what the feeling was. It was Jimmy.

The boys had made it to the top of the hill. It really was a beautiful view, just as Laurie had assured them it would be. The last of the sunlight reflecting off the water, the mountains in the distance, and the quiet.

Jimmy felt so tall. He was good at estimating, something he had learned in the math classes he took in school. He guessed they had to be at least 200 feet up from the lake and rocks below where he could no longer see it, but he knew his cousins' house was also situated.

He liked the feeling of looking down on everything. He didn't feel so different up there. The lake and air treated him the same as they would anyone else. The breeze rustling through his soft, brown curls and tickling his scalp, paying no mind to the size of the head it covered.

He stood still for some time, breathing slowly, his nerves calmer than he thought they had ever been.

He was so calm there, at the top of that hill, that he didn't see his cousins watching him, noticing how distracted he was, and then slowly slipping away back into the woods, leaving Jimmy alone at the top of the hill.

When Jimmy did finally realize they had gone, he paid no mind for a moment more, until he remembered he had followed his cousins through the woods to this spot, and was unsure of how to get back to their house.

"Jack?" he called out. "Matt?"

There was no response. The same breeze he had just felt gently whirling through his hair now turned into a strong wind, whistling in the bare trees above him. He was cold. He had forgotten how cold he was for that moment he spent overlooking the water.

The temperature was dropping and so was the sun. He could see the orange rays beginning to fade behind the mountains across the lake. He estimated that it was somewhere around forty-five degrees when they first set out from the house, but it was quickly becoming colder. The wind had started to stab at his bare skin.

"Jack? Matt?" he called out again. The wind was stronger now, louder. He made his way back into the woods, away from the cliff, hoping to escape some of the chill. He didn't know which way to go. They had walked a good distance to get to the top, he knew that. *Forty, fifty minutes?* he thought. He was unsure of just how long they had walked.

Jimmy was getting nervous again, really nervous.

"Jack! Matt!" he began frantically calling out.

He could no longer see the sun or the sky anymore under the cover of the woods. The frozen branches up ahead engulfed him, leaving nowhere for him to escape but within.

Jimmy started running, panicking, tears streaming down his face, and he shut his eyes. He felt nothing then, except for the weight of his feet on the hard, uneven ground.

Running straight, with his eyes shut, his foot slipped under a large, fallen branch, and he began to fall, tumbling forward.

It seemed to him that he would fall forever, the rest of his existence made up only of falling, helpless, blind.

He rolled down the hill which seemed so innocent on

his way up, but now felt like a monster entangling him. The branches scraping through his long-sleeved shirt, ripping up the skin on his arms. He could smell the leaves and dirt as he rolled down.

His forward motion was finally stopped by a large oak tree, with a trunk five feet wide. He was stopped as the back of his head hit the solid trunk, and he lay at the base, under the cover of the long, barren branches, unconscious.

Hours passed. The temperature dropped below twenty degrees, the wind only growing stronger, snow began to fall. Jimmy lay under the oak tree for hours, covered by soft snowflakes and dead branches blown down by the wind. It was early morning when he was found. He was still under the large oak tree, completely frozen with icicles stuck to his lashes, and his eyes shut tight.

# ACKNOWLEDGMENTS

The stories in this collection have appeared in slightly different forms in the following publications:

"Where You Will Find It" in the *Pine Hills Review*

"If One Afternoon Your Lover Says" in *After the Pause*

"Shrinking Space" in *Asymmetry* Magazine

I offer my thanks and appreciation to the editors of these publications for taking a chance on me.

My gratitude is also offered to the editors of Atmosphere Press and to my dear family and friends who have always and continue to extend the gift of their support and attention to my stories.

# ABOUT ATMOSPHERE PRESS

Atmosphere Press is an independent, full-service publisher for excellent books in all genres and for all audiences. Learn more about what we do at atmospherepress.com.

We encourage you to check out some of Atmosphere's latest releases, which are available at Amazon.com and via order from your local bookstore:

*Comfrey, Wyoming: Birds of a Feather,* a novel by Daphne Birkmyer
*Relatively Painless,* short stories by Dylan Brody
*Nate's New Age,* a novel by Michael Hanson
*The Size of the Moon,* a novel by E.J. Michaels
*The Red Castle,* a novel by Noah Verhoeff
*American Genes*, a novel by Kirby Nielsen
*Newer Testaments,* a novel by Philip Brunetti
*All Things in Time,* a novel by Sue Buyer
*Hobson's Mischief,* a novel by Caitlin Decatur
*The Black-Marketer's Daughter,* a novel by Suman Mallick
*The Farthing Quest,* a novel by Casey Bruce
*This Side of Babylon*, a novel by James Stoia
*Within the Gray,* a novel by Jenna Ashlyn
*Where No Man Pursueth,* a novel by Micheal E. Jimerson
*Here's Waldo,* a novel by Nick Olson
*Tales of Little Egypt,* a historical novel by James Gilbert
*For a Better Life,* a novel by Julia Reid Galosy
*The Hidden Life,* a novel by Robert Castle

# ABOUT THE AUTHOR

Danielle Epting has published her creative work in various online journals. She currently lives in Albany, NY where she received her MA from the University at Albany. When she's not writing, she can be found running or walking with her pup, Echo. This is her first short story collection.

CPSIA information can be obtained
at www.ICGtesting.com
Printed in the USA
BVHW032351160521
607527BV00005B/100